CHRONOS

THE ARRIVAL

PRANJAL SENGUPTA

Made with ♥ on the Notion Press Platform
www.notionpress.com

This book is dedicated to my parents and our respected Principal Sir, Mr. Sujoy Biswas, without whose constant support and encouragement, I would not have been able to write this story.

Contents

Acknowledgements

I would like to express my heartiest thanks to my parents, teachers, and my friends for encouraging me to write this book. I am grateful to my friend, Bedanta for designing the cover of this book.

Disclaimer

This is a work of fiction. Names, characters, businesses, events and incidents are the products of the author's imagination. Any resemblance to actual persons, living or dead, or actual events is purely coincidental.

Prologue

Well, if you are reading this, that means I have been successful. Let me explain. I think I have finally found a way to send messages between universes. You see, the incidents that I have described in my story have really happened to me and for me, it's the reality. However, if I have really been successful in sending this to another universe or possibly many other universes which is rather more probable in this case, you may find some historical references that I have mentioned or certain well-known facts that are written here to be a bit different from what you know. This is the result of the small differences in the outcomes of some events among different parallel universes which have caused great impacts later in the timelines. Maybe in your Universe, the Conquerors (mentioned later in the story) don't exist at all. In that case, this will seem nothing more than an ordinary story to you and you should consider yourself very very lucky. I am not really sure whether anyone would even read this or why I am even writing this. But hey, why do spaceship crews in movies record mission logs? I really don't want to bore you with the technical details of how I am sending this message now. Maybe someday I will. Maybe one day I will even be able to travel between universes and meet my other selves in this vast multiverse.

Just a word of caution - if you want to really understand my story, you must remember that almost nothing you know about time travel, parallel universes, and the nature of reality is true. Hence, don't be prejudiced about the rules of time travel. This is the story of how my life turned upside down. So, here we go...

CHAPTER ONE

The Last Day of my Normal Life

It was the day of my 10th-grade final examination. I had completed writing my first public examination and I was feeling quite good about my performance. The result was supposed to be declared within a month and I was a bit nervous about it. But my work was done. I could relax a bit. When I reached home, I got a call from an unknown number. Just a month before, I had taken part in a contest whose winners would get a chance to go on an excursion to the ICI (Indian Cosmological Institute). From a very young age, I dreamt of becoming an astrophysicist. So when I picked up the call, I was overwhelmed with joy when the man on the other end of the call informed me that I was one of the winners of the competition and had been selected for going on the excursion to the ICI. The excursion was supposed to take place the following week. And I received one of those fancy ICI Visitor lanyards through the mail the following day.

Since the ICI was located in Bengaluru and I lived in Kolkata, I had to take a flight to go there. My parents, after some trepidation, did allow me to travel alone, although I was not fully comfortable with their decision. Their reason was "You need to see the real world." Nevertheless, I too agreed.

So, the day before my departure, I started packing. That was the first thing I tried to do completely on my own which I soon realised was a complete disaster. I could not decide which items I should take. Everything seemed important. At last, it was my mom who came to my rescue and helped me pack my luggage which we finished by the night.

When we were having dinner that day, my father, who had travelled on a flight once before, gave me some instructions about how to board a plane and some tips if I ever had nausea or headache during the course of the journey. I could understand from his constant reassurance, "There's nothing to be afraid of..." that he himself was a bit afraid. After all, this was my first journey without my parents to some other state, that too on a plane.

The next day I had to wake up at 6 a.m. as the flight was scheduled to take off at 11 a.m. My parents had me taken to the Netaji Subhas Chandra Bose International Airport, Kolkata and we sat there for half an hour. To be honest, I was both excited as well as a bit nervous to board an aeroplane for the first time.

I saw a group of 6 or 7 teenagers, most of them of my age arriving. They were wearing ICI lanyards just like I was from which I deduced that they were also a part of the Kolkata team.

A few minutes later, there was an announcement made in the airport requiring the students going for the ICI excursion to form a line near counter 3. I bid my parents farewell and went to the specified area.

A tall guy was standing there, about the age of 25. He had curly and short black hair. He was wearing a black T-Shirt with the Euler's formula printed on it and a pair of circular steel-rimmed glasses. He first called out all our names, including mine, 'Aniruddha Sen' but he laid stress on the 'A' making my name sound like 'Aaa-niruddha Sen'. I could hear some of the other students giggling which kind of annoyed me.

The tall guy handed us our flight tickets and said to us, "Due to some unavoidable circumstances, our flight has been delayed by three hours. You guys can either stay here or you can leave, but don't forget to regroup at 1:30 p.m. sharp."

I thought of going for the latter option but I noticed that my parents had already left. Thus, I had no other choice but to wait there for the three hours. I saw that most of the members of the Kolkata Team were leaving. The few that had chosen to stay back were sitting together on a row of chairs at some distance. I thought of introducing myself to them, but seeing the way they were engrossed in their smartphones, I decided against it.

I was sitting alone watching my surroundings. Numerous people came to the airport every day. A man wearing a black suit with a black tie, holding a briefcase in one hand and yelling at someone on his phone, was hurrying to board his flight. A family with two kids, both around ten years old, had just landed and were leaving the airport. Two pilots came and sat behind me, having a sandwich, and one of them was boasting about how he landed an aeroplane once, after losing two of its three engines.

It was at this moment that I dozed off. I had the weirdest dream. I was sitting on an aeroplane. Suddenly some song which I had never heard in my life started playing. Although the plane was midair, both the pilot and the copilot, who were wearing hats and sunglasses for some reason, came out and started moonwalking on the aisle. I looked outside and the plane was taking an uncontrolled dive. Suddenly the song changed. But this time, I kind of recognised the tune. I saw the ground through the window getting bigger and bigger and as soon as the plane hit the ground, I woke up only to find that the last song that was playing in my dream was actually my ringtone which was playing on my phone as my mother was calling me. I told her the entire story about the flight delay and my dream.

She said, "Why didn't you call us? We were still nearby, we could have easily come back. Anyways, be careful and give me a call when you reach Bangalore."

I looked at my watch. It was 1:25 p.m. The other students had already started coming back. I went to the washroom to wash my face once as I had just woken up from a nightmare. I saw the Euler's formula T-Shirt guy waiting in front of Counter 3. Some students had also gathered there. I went there too. We were then shown the way to our flight and the aeroplane door was opened.

We boarded the aeroplane after the airport authorities scanned our luggage. It was a commercial flight, so there were several people other than the ones going on the excursion. I took out my phone and earphones from my bag and kept my luggage in one of the overhead bins above my designated seat. I got seat number 13. Although I do not believe in superstitions, I did not like that number. I can't really explain why. I noticed that seat 13 was the right one of two seats on the left side of the plane. That meant no window seat for me. Since the seat to my immediate left was still vacant, I swiftly shifted to that seat.

I had just put on my earphones and started playing my favourite playlist on my mobile when a girl of my age pulled it out from one of my ears. I was both startled and annoyed, the song still playing in my left ear. She was probably going to say, "Please get out of my seat," as I thought that was the only reason she might have had to interrupt me like that. But my face must have given such an expression that she stopped herself, giggled a little and sat down. I didn't say anything else.

She kept one of her luggage in the overhead bin, just beside mine while I continued playing songs until we were asked to turn off all electronic devices.

During the takeoff, our seats began to shake vigorously for some time during which I got extremely scared. The girl sitting beside me, who seemed to be perfectly fine, asked, "First time?" I nodded my head. She just smiled a bit while going through her bag for something.

The girl had straight black hair and was wearing a yellow T-shirt with the same ICI lanyard from which I concluded that she too was one of the members of the Kolkata Team.

After some time, when I was busy on my mobile, she exclaimed, "Look!" Outside, I could see my hometown Kolkata with all its buildings and streets filled with history and culture. I saw the famous yellow taxis which seemed like little ants spread across the entire city. It was the most amazing scene I had ever seen. So there I was, peacefully enjoying and appreciating the view on the last simple day of my life.

CHAPTER TWO

I Make a New Friend

I had almost fallen asleep when I felt someone calling me from the seat behind me. To my surprise, it was my friend Rahul. We used to go to school together, that is until he left our school in the seventh grade. We talked for a bit. He told me that he was going to Bengaluru to attend one of his cousin's weddings. Then the guy with the Euler's formula T-shirt came and announced that all the participants would be divided into teams of two; each team consisting of the participants who were sitting together on the plane.

I was reading an article on my mobile phone about a supposed UFO sighting when the girl sitting next to me spoke, "So, do you believe aliens really exist?"

To be honest I considered the answer to be quite obvious. There are numerous galaxies in the Universe, each of them containing millions and billions of stars. I think it's next to impossible that all of those planets should be devoid of life and incapable of harbouring it. So I told her what I believed.

She replied, "Yeah, of course, but... But how many of those life forms do you think are intelligent like us or even more than us? What do you think?" I smiled and answered, "That's quite a question, isn't it?"

After some time, the girl held out her hand and told me her name - Anita Banerjee. I, too, introduced myself. After that, we started talking about our schools, our favourite subjects and other topics. I came to know we both had the same dream of becoming an astrophysicist. We both being science nerds, exchanged some ideas about astrophysics and quantum physics. After about half an hour the flight attendant came up and asked if we were vegetarian or not. We both promptly answered that we weren't. I didn't like vegetarian food and the way she replied, it was quite clear that she didn't like it either. Then we all had our lunch. The meal was extremely delicious, but nobody could deny that the water that was provided tasted funny, to say the least.

After we had had our meal, I kept on watching the scenes outside the window. I even captured some of it on my phone camera just to show it to my parents later. It was like Wordsworth's lines "I gazed-and gazed-but little thought..." However, this gazing was soon making me light-headed. So I stopped.

CHAPTER THREE

I Ruin an Excursion

Soon after, Anita asked me, "Does anything feel strange here?" She was going to say something else but she stopped as soon as the tall guy came. He asked all of us, "Any problem, guys?" We said together, "No Sir." We then saw him entering a cabin behind us. After looking around a bit, Anita asked me, "Did you see his badge?" I didn't understand. Why would she suddenly mention a man's badge? Although she said it was nothing, I could understand something was troubling her.

It was nearly 5 o'clock when we arrived at our destination. However, since it was already late in the evening, we were made to enter a hotel nearby that day. But we were assured that visiting the ICI would be the first thing the next morning.

While entering our rooms, I noticed that every teammate was assigned rooms next to each other. Since Anita's room was next to mine, we chatted in my room for some time planning our visit to the ICI the next day. I sometimes regret making any plans as I know things NEVER go according to plans, but this time I made an exception as both of us were too excited. She went to her room. After having a phone call with my mom, I fell asleep. I was really worried that I would not be able to wake up at the proper time the next day, as I am extremely lazy and at home, I often oversleep and only wake up if my parents wake me up.

The next day, after waking up, and checking my mobile phone, I realised that my nightmares had come true. I HAD OVERSLEPT. We were supposed to leave at 8 but I woke up at 8:30. Suddenly, I heard the sound of someone banging on the door so hard that I prayed that it would not break.

I was quite sure that it was the hotel authorities trying to vacate me from the room. But to my surprise, when I opened the door, a boy was standing there, probably of my age or perhaps a bit older; I couldn't figure that out. He was wearing a casual blue T-shirt, matching the colour of his trousers which seemed a bit odd as I was wearing a similar dress the previous day at home. He asked me extremely sarcastically, "Why the hell did you set your alarm to ring at 7 p.m.?"

I got really annoyed and went to check my phone, only to find that he was telling the truth. Phew! At least it wasn't that I did not wake up even after hearing the alarm; still, it didn't make the incident less embarrassing for me. But when I asked him how he knew that, he said it didn't matter and to follow his instructions very carefully.

I was a bit scared and hesitant due to his kind of eccentric nature at first, but when he told me that he was from the future, I was relieved to conclude that he was a total lunatic. When he realised that I was not taking him seriously, he just stopped and said, "Where's Anita?"

I didn't say anything but I could get a premonition that he would then say something troubling. He said, "Haven't you met her yet?" to which I did not reply. He then murmured to himself, walking around my room in circles. I interrupted his thoughts saying that she probably had already left for the ICI. He hurriedly went out. I stayed in the room, but after some time, he came back and gave me a very annoying look. He then told me to get dressed up and follow him. I had no other choice but to do so. I had to go to the ICI anyways, and apologise to Anita. So I decided to go with him. What was the worst that could happen? I get to travel with a madman, I thought to myself. Moreover, there was something quite familiar about him. It was as if a part of me kind of already trusted him.

We went outside after checking out of the hotel. I was told by the guard that a girl was looking for me. I was quite sure it was my teammate Anita, who would probably kill me when she saw me again, I thought. Although I suspected that the boy would again be triggered when he heard that, he did not seem to react. He just asked me whether I had any money with me.

I had 2000 rupees with me, but I told him that I had only 50 rupees as I was a bit sceptical. He made us get into a local bus. When we seated ourselves, I asked him, "By the way, where do you think we're going?" He answered, "The ICI, to rescue her. You and I have a lot to catch up on."

I was totally confused. I might seem a bit childish but I really hoped that he was rescuing me from the embarrassing situation that I had brought upon myself by oversleeping that day. It seemed a bit fishy, but if he really was a time traveller, he could surely have come a bit earlier to wake me up at the proper time. But watching his behaviour since the morning, I thought it was better not to raise that particular question at the moment.

I was also wondering why Anita would be in trouble. Was it because her teammate was too lazy to be on time? Seeing me thinking to myself he said, "I know it's been a rough day but you have to trust me. The fate of the entire world lies in our hands. I am from the future - a terrible one. We need to fix it. I know you don't believe me..." "Of course, I don't believe you," I protested, "Would you believe a guy who just showed up on your door and said 'I am from the future... Help me save the world'? No, I don't..." He didn't even let me finish and just shouted at me, "Please let me finish!", this time quite seriously, so much so that I felt like I got a scolding from my parents.

He then continued, "I have been sent here to make sure that the future that I am from does not come into being. In my time, Earth is overrun by a war unlike anything in the past. Soon, there will be an alien attack. Humans will get help from another benevolent alien species but still, they will lose. So, in my time, I was created by some of the most intelligent minds in human history with technology provided by the benevolent alien race - The Designers. They have helped shape humanity since it came into being. I have been sent here because today's the day the war actually begins." I was speechless. But the slightly awkward thing was that the other passengers of the bus were speechless too - even the driver who had stopped midway to listen to our story. The boy yelled at him and the bus started moving again. I asked him what he meant by 'He was created'. He fumbled a bit when I asked him if he was a robot. "Well yes and no. It's complicated", he replied. He didn't even bother to answer my question about how I was involved in this.

We got off the bus and stopped at the gates of the ICI. He said to me, "Go in, find Anita and meet me here in

5 minutes." I asked why he didn't do it himself. He just pointed his finger at my lanyard and smiled sarcastically.

I went in and was told that the team was in the observatory. I could see Anita having much fun learning the workings of a telescope. I was both embarrassed and a bit jealous as I always wanted to use one. Well so much for rescuing her. I thought I had to wait till the entire demonstration was finished. But she saw me through the glass doors and came out. "What the hell were you doing? I was shouting in front of your room", she whispered to me, but in such a tone that I felt she would hit me at any moment. I explained the entire thing to her, but in her shoes, even I would think that my story was completely bogus. And of course, she did too.

"You are either a terrible liar or completely out of your mind," she said, "You know, just leave it. Let's go."

I kind of agreed with her but then I remembered that the boy knew her name too and that she was my teammate, so I wanted Anita to at least meet him. Maybe she knew him, I thought. After telling this to Anita, she rolled her eyes and said, "Fine! Let's go meet your new friend."

CHAPTER FOUR

BULLETS FIRED

We were walking towards the exit when I saw the boy, running and shouting, “Got it! Got it! Now find another exit!” I was going to ask something, perhaps the fact why two armed guards were chasing him but then I noticed one of them prepping his gun. I ran like my life depended on it. Oh! It really did. I noticed that there was a sign pointing towards another exit. I took the left corridor as indicated when I heard a gunshot. I froze. Although I didn’t quite know either of the two who were being chased, I was extremely relieved to see them behind me, taking the turn to the corridor. But my relief dissolved into fear when I saw the two guards, now both of them holding guns in their hands, chasing the three of us. Still, what I didn’t know was why we were being chased. But it didn’t seem to matter then, as the guards looked like ‘Shoot-first-ask-question-later’ kind of guys.

I almost made it to the exit when the boy shouted, “Not that one! Follow me.” He was running while looking at a black hemispherical device he was holding in his hand. He smashed open a door, completely ignoring the "Authorised Personnel Only” sign written clearly in large, bold letters on the door. He closed and locked the door by putting the broom kept beside it in between the handles of the door.

My jaw dropped as soon as I saw the thing that was now staring at me. He really was telling the truth. There wasn't any other explanation. Before me, was a gigantic spaceship. It was pitch black and triangular in shape. It was hovering about 2 metres above the ground and there did not seem to be any entrance, that is until the boy went towards it and a small black disc detached from the centre of its triangular base and lowered itself down to the ground.

Suddenly we heard a bang! The guards had broken the door. Now there were five of them, all carrying guns. The odd thing was that they were being led by the guy in black T-Shirt who had travelled with us. He was carrying a different type of gun; I had never seen anything like that before in my life. They started shooting at us.

The boy and I made it onto the platform but Anita was not so lucky. A bullet hit Anita in her left hand. At once, she gave out a cry and fell down on the ground. I rushed back to her. The boy also ran towards her. The guards were still shooting at us. She somehow grabbed my arm with her right hand. We picked her up and somehow reached the platform without any of us getting shot again.

Once we boarded the ship, the boy immediately went to the controls at the front of the bridge of the ship. The interior walls of the ship, which was previously pitch black just like the exterior, lit up bright white and the front part of the bridge became transparent. The boy, still managing the controls of the ship shouted, "Take her to the med bay! Fast!" But I didn't know where it was and seeing the condition he was in, desperately trying to take off, I could hardly ask for directions. I couldn't leave Anita either. Her arm was bleeding; it seemed like she would pass out at any moment. I thought if I could somehow stop the bleeding,

I could go and search for the med bay and then take her there. I tore off one of the sleeves of my T-shirt and wrapped it tightly around the wound. She looked away, trying hard not to cry out in pain. But I felt there was no other way. "I'm coming in a minute," I said. She didn't reply. She couldn't.

After going around almost the entire ship, I found the med bay. I ran back to where I left Anita. She was still there, sitting on the table in one corner. I took her slowly to the med bay. She could barely walk. Thankfully, the devices there were fully automated. She lay down on one of the MedBeds and the device automatically switched itself on. A semicircular thing scanned her and unwrapped the tourniquet I had made. It pushed an injection into her left arm just beside the wound. But she didn't notice it. The pain of the wound was much greater. Soon she began to relax. She went from being short of breath to being quite calm. An automated robotic arm took out the bullet. Suddenly there was a jolt in the spaceship. It was so intense that the bullet dropped from the grip of the arm and fell on the floor. The ship finally took off. Then another robotic arm took the place of the previous one which stitched the wound. But it was not any ordinary stitch that you may have had during any injury. It seemed as if the device used some laser-like light rays to regrow skin and muscle cells at and near the wound.

Anita was sleeping quite peacefully now that the wound was closed. I was sitting just beside her when I heard footsteps behind me. It was the boy.

To be honest, I was furious with him. Both Anita and I had trusted him even after he ruined our excursion and in turn, his recklessness got Anita shot. If only he had told us what he was going to do; that he would steal the key to the ship or whatever that glowing device in his hand was, or that armed guards in 'shoot-to-kill' mode would be chasing us for something he did, we would have been prepared, or even better - we would have stayed away.

I somehow managed not to hit him in the face. Still, I gave him a piece of my mind. This time, instead of shouting back, he just quietly listened to me.

After I finished what I had to say, he asked me to give him the bullet that hit Anita. He said he needed to check something. By then, Anita had woken up due to all my shouting. She was trying to get up but both of us forbade her to do so and advised her to take rest for some time. I gave him the bullet as he asked. I went towards Anita. She was still lying down on the MedBed but was now awake. She said to me, not directly looking at me, "Thank you, uhh... you know, for saving me. Not many would have done that." Then she took a quick glance at me. "How are you feeling?" I asked. "Better," she said. Suddenly, the boy interrupted our exchange and said "No." "What do you mean 'No'?" I said. The boy, examining the bullet now said, his voice almost breaking, "She isn't getting better. She's not going to." Tears rolled down his face. He continued, "It's time you both knew the whole truth."

CHAPTER FIVE

All Hail the Designers

Anita got up. "What do you mean? I am fine," she said. She tried to stand but immediately sat down again. "Just lost my balance, huh", she said, smiling it off. Then the boy started speaking. "As I told you, " he said, looking at me, "from the future I am from, there was an alien invasion. Billions of people died. You have to first get this, humans are NOT alone in the Universe, nor are they the most intelligent species, no matter what most of them think. There are far more advanced species, some of them are pacifists and peaceful, while others know only to destroy other civilisations. One of these destructive species is the beings from the planet Krates. We call them the Conquerors. They are one of the most dangerous species in the entire Universe. Once they land on a planet, they start infecting individuals, taking control of their entire mind and body, using it to infect its next target."

"You mean, like a virus," I said. "No, he said, "Not at all. Viruses do not have a mind. They don't choose whom to infect and when to infect. The Conquerors take control of the host's mind too, hijacking its brain and getting all the information from it, essentially resulting in the person itself becoming a Conqueror with nothing but a remnant of the original consciousness. And they have a hive mind. So all of them remain connected. They have destroyed hundreds of planets just like the Earth. Thus, to stop them, a few million years ago, The Designers sent one million of their soldiers to eradicate the Conquerors. The battle between the two alien species, which took place in this very solar system, lasted a thousand Earth years and after numerous casualties of the Designers, they finally won, or so they thought at the time. The thirty-two of them that survived the war returned to the other side of the galaxy, to their home planet, Entown, only to find that during the course of the battle, some Conquerors had escaped and destroyed their planet. They returned to the battle site to check if they had missed any Conqueror, but they couldn't find any. Then they found you, the humans who were nothing but a newborn species back then - just starting to form a civilisation on the Earth. The remaining Designers pledged to protect the planet and all its inhabitants from any hostile alien species that may threaten their existence, and they have done so successfully for more than two million years."

He stopped for a bit, looked at Anita, and frowned. His face expressed deep sorrow and defeat, like he had failed. I asked him, "But why? Why do these Conquerors go on destroying planets?" "For achieving victory over other species. They want to be the only species in the Universe," he said, "The Designers had developed the technology to detect any active Conqueror here, on the Earth. They didn't find any for a long time. But the Conquerors were hiding in plain sight, passing from the individuals from one generation to the next, each time gathering as much information as it could. But this time they just chose to do it ever so subtly. They did not hijack the host's brain, allowing it to live a normal life, and pass a conqueror on to the next generation. It, like everything else, had evolved. Today almost all humans contain a conqueror inside them - you two included."

I was really scared but he saw my facial expression and continued, "Don't worry they are dormant, at least the one inside you is." He looked down, disappointed. Anita and I looked at each other. I kind of began to understand what had just happened, and my fears came true when the boy continued, "The bullet... The bullet that hit you contained an activator."

All of us became silent. Then Anita spoke, with a breaking voice, from trying to hide the fear and helplessness she was feeling, "There are worse ways of dying, I guess." She was looking at me, hopeless.

"Oh no, you won't die," the boy said, "the Conqueror won't kill you. It will do something much worse. It will make you watch every horrible thing it uses you to do. I have seen best friends kill each other with their own hands. I have seen..." He was holding back tears. He rushed out muttering something to himself.

In my entire life, I never quite really have had a friend with whom I could really connect. I didn't really find anyone who was like me. So, when I met Anita, I really thought she and I would have been best friends. If any other person would have told this story about these Conquerors to us, I would surely have handed him over to the police, but it's kind of hard to do that when you're in a spaceship, that too which belongs to the person who told you the story. Nothing really seemed impossible at the time.

I said to Anita, "Don't worry, I will stay here." "No," she said, "If what he said is really true; that the Conqueror inside me would... might make me take anyone's life, stay away from me, please..." She broke down. "I don't want to kill anyone, I don't... I don't want to die..." She was looking at me; her eyes gave out a feeling of trust and desperation. I felt guilty. If only I had listened to her and had gone with her to the observatory, she would have been fine. It was my fault, I dragged her into this mess. Still, I reassured her that everything would be alright and that I was not going anywhere. But what could an ordinary boy from Kolkata do when a person who had future technology at his disposal had given up hope?

Suddenly I saw it. Both her hands and feet had turned blue. Afraid that the Conqueror might have become fully active, I moved back a bit and called the boy, shouting so loud that he came running.

He saw the same thing that I did, but instead of giving a horrified look on his face like me, he felt relieved and excited and a bit surprised. He said, gasping for breath due to all the excitement, "I will be needing your blood to confirm it, but..." "But what?" we both exclaimed. "How much time does she have?" I pessimistically asked. "Why so negative," he said, "I think she made it, at least this time."

We were both surprised. He had just told us that there was no cure for it. But how could she survive now that the Conqueror had already been activated? When asked this question, he answered, now looking at Anita who was perplexed, "I think you have a Designer gene that killed the Conqueror. The blue colour is due to parts of the killed Conqueror flowing through your circulatory system. It will be fully removed within some time. You just need a few hours of rest and you'd be fit as a fiddle."

We were speechless, but the boy seemed ready to jump with excitement. But, he calmed himself down and hurriedly took out a device from one of the racks in the med bay. It looked kind of like those digital thermometers, but instead of a mercury bulb, it had a needle."

Anita was looking at me, smiling. The dreadful look in her eyes turned into one of gleeful excitement. She couldn't be happier. After all, she had just killed one of the most dangerous beings in the Universe. She was going to say something to me when the boy pricked her left arm with the needle. She almost hit the boy due to the sudden prick but he couldn't care less.

He was overwhelmed with joy while looking at the device screen and said, "Yep! I was right. You are one of the descendants of one of the remaining Designers and he just saved you. As far as I know, the Designers who survived the extinction did so only due to a mutation they developed due to prolonged exposure to the Sun. It seems the mutation is inheritable." He quickly took out the needle of the device, broke it, and discarded it, while he kept the device back where it originally was. He rushed back to us and said, smiling and clasping his hands together, "Now let's get back to saving the world, shall we?"

CHAPTER SIX

I FLY A SPACESHIP

Suddenly we felt a jolt. The entire spaceship seemed to shake vigorously and the lights flickered. The boy said, "I take it back, first we have to get out of here." The boy rushed back to the control centre. I followed but told Anita to stay in the MedBed and take rest, although I wasn't sure if she could really rest with all the shaking that was going on in the ship.

The entire wall of the bridge had now become transparent leaving only a small part of the wall opaque and backlit with white lights, where the entrance to the bridge was present. I saw two fighter jets, like those they have in the air force, chasing us and shooting us. The boy was standing in front of me desperately trying to get out of the place. "Hey, the walls are transparent, can they see us," I asked. "No," he answered, "it's one-way. Take a seat and help me, will you?"

I was wondering whether he had forgotten that there was no seat or he was asking me to sit on the floor, when a chair appeared right in front of me. I sat down slowly and carefully, being sceptical. Hey, for all I knew, it might have been an illusion! Surprisingly and thankfully, it wasn't. But what perplexed me even more, was that as soon as I sat down, the controls in front of us vanished into thin air and a small different type of panel appeared in front of my chair. The white chair extended on both sides and also upwards to form a transparent screen in front of me. The boy said rather calmly, "Fly the ship. The Anti-Grav Core has been damaged. I have to go and repair it. In the meantime, try not to get hit by those jets and please don't crash." Yeah, how hard could it be? I placed my hands on the flat white control panel that seemed to remain in front of my chair without any support. The place where I kept my hands lit up, and it seemed that the ship was responding to both my thoughts and the movements of my hands. Both the screen in front of me and a voice said, "Welcome back, Captain." It seemed I was flying the ship so well that it mistook me for its captain, I thought to myself.

Suddenly the white lights of the floor and the part of the wall that was still opaque turned red and the voice said, "Shield strength is at twenty per cent. Destruction imminent in T-minus one minute." That genuinely frightened me. "Did you hear that," I yelled, hoping that the boy would now do something heroic and save the day. But he just said, "Working on it. One problem at a time." I heard the sound of some things dropping on the floor when he cried out, "For the Grand Designer's sake, can you just keep the ship still?" I replied, "Yeah, you try escaping from three fighter jets while keeping the ship stable. And who's the Grand Designer?"

He didn't reply. I noticed Anita coming from the med bay. I told her to go back, but she was too busy appreciating the view outside, that is until she saw the fighter jets trying to shoot us down. She was coming towards my chair when one of the missiles hit the ship. She almost fell down, when a chair appeared out of nowhere exactly where she was standing and prevented her from falling down on the floor. The voice said, "Shields at five per cent. Evacuation advised." It was starting to become really annoying.

Then there was a glimmer of hope when it said, "Anti-Grav is now fully operational." The lights on the panel turned blue. I moved my hand forward and suddenly we were going up and up and up, leaving the fighter jets far behind, above the atmosphere. The weird thing is that we didn't feel the acceleration like the one when you fall backwards when a bus starts suddenly. I continued steering the ship upwards till the sky became pitch black and I could see the stars. Most of the ship wall went opaque leaving only a small part of the front still transparent. The lights went back from red to white again. "Shields recharging. No imminent threat detected," the voice said. I sighed in relief.

I looked back only to see Anita sitting on the chair which had suddenly appeared to catch her and the boy walking towards us. "Did you see that? I flew a spaceship. A spaceship," I exclaimed. The boy said, "You certainly did. Now, let's..." Anita got up from her seat and walked towards the part of the wall which had become transparent. I stood up too. As soon as I did, the control panel disappeared and so did the chair and the controls reappeared at the very front part of the spaceship just like it was when we had first entered the spaceship. It still had the same design. But now it was attached to the front transparent wall of a spaceship instead of hovering above the floor and almost resembled a table. And this time there were some buttons with white outlines on the panel, like the ones on a touchscreen.

I looked above. It was a magnificent sight indeed. I had flown the ship to such an altitude while fleeing from the fighter jets chasing us that I had almost reached the Moon. I mean I had seen the Moon with a telescope before but seeing it in real life, up close, with all its craters and dark spots was mesmerising. The boy touched a button on the panel and the floor became transparent too. That seemed to scare the hell out of Anita and me. We both almost jumped up thinking that the floor was gone. But when we looked down, we saw an even more beautiful view. It was the Earth. I know there are many pictures of the Earth taken from outer space available on the Internet, but seeing it with my own eyes was a different feeling altogether. I felt so large and small at the same time, if that makes sense. I had lived my whole life on that planet. I hadn't even explored the entire world. When I was on the planet, I felt that it was a great big world like most of you do. But seeing it from above, all at once - day and night at the same time, all those people living their lives on that blue sphere, the Earth felt so small now, so delicate.

Suddenly, the boy interrupted, "Uhh, if you have finished appreciating the view, we have a job to do. We have to save the world if you remember." We all gathered in the centre of the room. The boy told us to sit down and three seats appeared just like before.

Now there appeared in front of us a triangular table with each seat placed next to each side of the triangle. The boy said, "The war with the Conquerors starts today. The men who were chasing us, the Conquerors in their bodies, had already been activated before. These three are their leaders."

He showed us pictures of two men and a woman. The man with the black Euler's formula T-Shirt guy was one of them. "That's what bugged me," Anita said, "They are all military personnel." "Not only that, if you really are the descendant of a Designer, you should have felt their presence; that something was wrong," said the boy. Anita said, surprised and excited, "Yeah, I did! It was a feeling I had never experienced in my entire life. But what was he doing on a children's excursion?" "That might have been my fault," the boy said. He went on, "Well, while landing this spaceship here, I kind of crashed and the ICI took custody of it. I barely escaped after encrypting the instructions of the mission that were given to me. I might have uhh... forgotten to encrypt the names of the people I was supposed to meet." He pointed his fingers towards the both of us. "That's why their Queen decided to keep a close eye on you two," he said.

I gave him an angry look but Anita did not seem to react much. The guy was named Anand Hazra and the other two were Scott Hands and Elizabeth Morrison. The boy went on, "And this is why we don't have much time. This guy, Anand Hazra is their Queen. And the only way to win this war is to kill the Queen before she chooses her successor. That is their only vulnerability - if their Queen dies without a successor, the hive mind will separate into individual consciousnesses and they won't be able to survive for longer than two years. And now, thanks to us, the Queen knows that something is up. So she might make her choice for her successor as soon as tomorrow." I said, "But if you are telling this to us and preventing the end of the world, doesn't that mean you no longer travel back to save the world as it has already been saved and cause its destruction again? The whole thing becomes a paradox." The boy replied with a smile, "Actually it doesn't. The irony is that you yourself will discover this after a few years." I became really excited on hearing this. "You are already familiar with the three dimensions of space in this universe. But there are many universes in the multiverse, and almost all of the universes exist in clusters of parallel universes. The multiverse itself is a fifth-dimensional structure having four spatial dimensions and the other dimension being time itself. What you perceive as time can be traversed just like space if you exist outside the universe, in the inter-universal space." His face glowed with excitement even when explaining my theory of time and the multiverse to us. He continued, "According to your theory, at the end of the universe, dark energy loses the fight to gravity and starts the Big Crunch. The universe which had been expanding first starts slowing down and then starts contracting. Ultimately, the entire universe becomes a single dense point resulting in the next Big Bang, starting the next universal cycle."

"Then, is it just one big bang or are there multiple parallel universes? Got a bit confused," I said, smiling. "Well, kind of both," he said, "the transition from the Big Crunch to the Big Bang exists as a single moment in time, and it links all the parallel universes together. In your theory, you called it the Nexus. If you could see all the five dimensions from the inter-universal space, you would see almost an infinite number of parallel universes appear like rings with all of them touching a single point. Think of a doughnut but shrink its hole so much that it becomes a point. That is the Nexus, with all the parallel universes like the outlines of the circular slices of the doughnut, that is if you cut it like a pizza... Anyways..."

"But that means we don't have free will. All our actions are prewritten and are pre-decided according to the Universe we are in right now," I interrupted. "Or the other way round," said Anita, "You can also say the actions we take and the choices we make determine the Universe we are in." "Exactly," said the boy, "The weird thing about the cluster of parallel universes is that you can't determine which universe you are in without leaving your own universe and going into another, and even if you do that, it just creates a number of copies of the universe you travelled into and the universe you left, based on the decision you will take in the new universe you just entered, creating the same dilemma of free will once again."

There was a schematic representation of what he was saying, visible above the table like a hologram. "But how did you travel through time? Are you, like, from this universe or did you travel across the multiverse to get here," I enquired.

"Neither actually," he continued, "I kind of lied when I said I am from the future." I got up from the chair as I was getting really annoyed with his cryptic 'kind of lies'. He told me to sit down and said, "I am not from the future but from a future. In my universe, on the last day of humanity, this spaceship was modified to survive the Big Crunch and pass through the Nexus and was sent into deep space away from the Earth. Since the Nexus is common for every parallel universe, my theory was that if I could pass through the Nexus and the Big Crunch, I would... to be very precise a copy of me would enter through every Big Bangs into every universe's beginning into the next universal cycle. I call this process Injection. The nice thing in this process is that only information gets passed on to the successive universes, not matter or energy, so it does not violate the laws of conservation."

If what he was telling us was the truth, and I strongly believed it was, then he had been waiting for this day since the beginning of this universe. On asking him about this, he answered, "Well, you'll find out in a few years. Why should I spoil the future?" He smiled and giggled. "Enough about me. You need to know the plan now," he said, now in a grave tone.

He continued, "In my Universe, we discovered some relics, embodiments of different aspects of the Universe itself. And the surprising thing is that they are sentient. They can judge their bearer. If, and only if they consider their bearer to be worthy, they will change into a form which can be worn by the bearer. For example, if it's a human, the relic transforms into a ring. We found three of them, giving the bearer control over space, time and knowledge respectively. The three of them, when used together, could grant an insane amount of power to any being, but only with the consent of their bearers. The Designers knew that if the Conquerors got their hands on any one of them, it was game over. Since the three relics were connected, once we found one of them, it wasn't too late before we succeeded in preventing the other two from falling into the hands of the Conquerors. But, the thing we didn't know, and the reason we failed was that there was one more relic - The Relic of Despair, we called it. We didn't actually know what the relic did but one thing was for sure – it turned any living being in its sight into a Conqueror. The Conquerors did something to it that completely destroyed its sentience. It only responded to the beck and call of the Conquerors. We only saw that on the last day of humanity. That day even the Designers fell. And once they did, there was hardly any hope left for the humans."

All of us were silent for some time. The boy's eyes were fixed on the white table. Anita asked in a low voice, "So what do we do now?"

The boy looked at both of us and smiled a bit like you do when you suddenly remember a happy memory. He then went on, "So the plan is really simple. Get the three relics and destroy the fourth."

"Yeah, so simple, isn't it," I said sardonically.

"Yeah, it is so simple. I happen to know the places where the relics of this universe are hidden," he said proudly. He stood up and so did we. He waved his hand and all the chairs and the table in between vanished. He then said, "So who's up for an adventure?"

CHAPTER SEVEN

THE DUNGEON OF THE SILENT MONKS

The boy went towards the controls of the ship and the ship started to rotate until we directly faced the Earth.

"Where are we going," both Anita and I enquired.

"A hidden place," he said, "Where we'll get the Relic of Time. Seat yourselves. Here we go!"

Two chairs appeared in front of us. We both sat down. The boy slided up one of the controls. The wall lights turned blue. The Earth first seemed to go a bit farther and then suddenly we were hurtling towards it. I could see my homeland, India. But instead of going towards my hometown, we went a bit north, towards the Himalayas, when suddenly the spaceship became parallel to the ground. The boy was manoeuvring the spaceship quite well, avoiding the peaks of the mountains.

Anita kept on shouting at the top of her voice, "Look out... We're gonna crash... Hey, hey, hey... We're gonna die..." Although I wasn't expressing it much, at every turn and bend, I had a mini heart attack. Still, I was enjoying the thrill.

We finally landed at the foot of a mountain. The boy went out of the bridge. We followed only to see him standing near a circle, which opened to reveal the platform through which we first boarded the ship.

All of us stepped on the platform and we were immediately being lowered down onto the ground. But as soon as it did, I immediately regretted stepping on it. It was freezing cold outside, and both Anita and I were shivering. The boy seemed to be quite fine. Perks of being a robot, I thought. I didn't have one of my sleeves too, which I had torn off to make a tourniquet for Anita.

It was snowing. I was hugging myself tightly, desperately trying to conserve my body heat. The boy shouted, "This way!" But his voice sounded like a divine instruction as he seemed nothing but a faint silhouette to my eyes. Nevertheless, I followed him. I looked behind me to make sure Anita was still following us. She was a bit farther away, so I screamed in the direction I had last seen the boy and told him to wait for Anita. I didn't know if he could really hear me, but I still decided to wait for her to catch up with me. She was shivering too. We kept on walking in the same direction for about five minutes, but we soon realised that we were lost. The boy was nowhere to be seen. I mean, even if he was standing ten feet away from us, the heavy snowfall would have made it impossible for us to see him and for him to see us.

Suddenly, Anita said, "Do you hear that?" I thought she was hallucinating and told her the same. "No no, I'm quite sure of it. There's music coming from there," she said, pointing a bit towards my right. "Come on," she grabbed my arm. She was running and I was forced to do the same as not doing so would result in the both of us falling face down on the ground.

We soon arrived in front of a huge door-like structure made of stone. There were some markings on it, which as soon as Anita touched, the door began to make a crackling noise. It started moving towards the right. We got in as soon as there was a space large enough for us to pass through. We didn't even care about what was inside as the cold had become unbearable by then. Both my palms and toes had already become numb.

But the problem was that the door was still opening, letting in all the snow and the icy-cold wind. As soon as it was fully opened, it started to close again. But we could not see the boy anywhere and as soon as I had this thought, when the door was about to shut off the wind completely, the boy came running and somehow managed to sneak in.

Seeing us, freezing due to the cold he said, "Oh! I should probably have given you the jackets." Both Anita and I gave him a sharp look while he laughed and gave us a mild apology.

There was not much heat inside but it wasn't bitterly cold like outside either. It was like an entrance to a cave. The roof was full of icicles which could only be seen due to a faint orangish-yellow light reflecting off a wall at a turn at some distance. We started to walk towards it.

We turned left to see where the light was coming from, but we saw something even stranger than finding a secret doorway inside a mountain in the first place. Eight people who resembled Buddhist monks, four on each side, were bowing down as if to greet our arrival. The passage led to a circular gateway which gave way to a flight of stairs finally leading to the bottom of a dungeon that was filled with monks too. The ceiling was like a dome and was full of beautiful patterns and designs. Twelve fire lanterns were hanging from the walls encircling the chamber and equidistant from each other. The monks were wearing blue robes instead of the traditional burgundy red ones, though they looked kind of green due to the flame.

We got down the stairs and the crowd parted to reveal a painting of a girl who seemed very familiar but I couldn't completely recognise. But as soon as I looked at Anita, I realised it. It was her. The face looked a bit older than Anita, but it was definitely hers. That was probably the reason the monks were bowing to her. I tried asking one of them why and how her face was on the painting, but he didn't answer. I looked at the boy who was smiling. It was clear that he knew what was going on, but he seemed to enjoy our astonishment and confusion.

Suddenly, a monk came out of the crowd. He was a bit older than the others and wore white robes. "I am afraid he won't be able to answer your question, my child," he said, "They have taken the vow of silence. They have travelled the whole world in search of you." He looked at Anita and continued, "And yet here you are! Their vow and this place our great leader had chosen have helped us to remain a secret for nearly a hundred years."

But that didn't answer my question. Anita too was spellbound to find her portrait in a secret dungeon in the Himalayas.

"But I heard music coming from here," said Anita. The monk said, "The Relic was calling to you."

"Come, sit," he said, "You are looking for the Relic of Time, I presume?" We nodded our heads. "Well," he said, "I have been its protector for the last forty years since its last bearer died. But before he did, he had a vision of a girl. The Relic had chosen its next bearer. He also told us the exact date when you would arrive here. Our great leader knew that he wouldn't live long enough to pass it on to his successor. So he made a painting of the girl in his vision and entrusted me with his responsibilities. I have been following his instructions ever since his death. I have sent emissaries to find you but they had no luck. But I had faith that you would come today just like he said. We were right to have been prepared for the ceremony."

I was still looking at the painting. The resemblance was really striking. Anita said to the monk, "What ceremony?"

"The Relic has already chosen who will be its next bearer," the monk answered, "But it also has to check whether it's the right time for you to have it."

Anita said, "What if it isn't? We need it now." "If it isn't the right time, then you can stay here with us. We can teach you how to use the Relic, or specifically, how not to use it," he said with a smile on his face.

"I don't think that would be necessary," the boy assured Anita. The monk looked at him. He studied him for some time and then slowly walked towards him. "The Relic gives certain abilities to the people around it, especially when it doesn't have a bearer," the monk said, "You are not of this time, are you?" The boy ignored the question and said, "Let's get on with the ceremony." The monk looked at Anita who nodded his head. "As you will," he bowed towards Anita and went back to the portrait. There was a golden plate with a red cloth covering something placed on it. He lifted the cloth and revealed a black irregular stone. It seemed quite ordinary. I really hoped that it wasn't one of the things that were going to save the world.

The monk brought it towards Anita. "Let the silence be broken and the ceremony begin," announced the monk. Anita stood up. The other monks who were present in the place started singing. It was like a hymn, in a language I didn't really recognise. As soon as the song started, there was a faint yellowish glow in the stone. It was as if a fire was kindled at the very centre of the stone and the stone became translucent to give way to the light.

As Anita reached for the stone, the glow began to grow brighter and brighter, until it became so bright that I couldn't look at it any longer. But Anita stared at it continuously without blinking even once. I looked away, but the brightness continued to go up. It seemed as though sunlight was entering the dungeon somehow. I had to close my eyes before the light blinded me. When I felt that the intensity was beginning to decrease, I opened one of my eyes just to be sure it was safe and then opened them both. Anita was standing there with a ring in her hand. It was a black shiny ring, with a perfectly circular groove running in the middle. Anita examined it for a moment and wore it on her finger. It gave out a pulse of faint yellow light which faded away very quickly.

"It seems that you were right," the monk said to the boy, "The ring has accepted its bearer." He looked at Anita and continued, "I would advise you to stay here for some time and learn how to use the ring but I feel a sense of urgency here. I wish you well on your journey and may the Relic guide you always."

The crowd of monks parted to make way for us back to the stairs. Anita and the boy went towards the stairway. I was going to follow them when the monk grabbed my hand. He said to me quietly and almost mindlessly,

"*The Bearer of Time, if thou deceive,*
Torment and Death thou shall receive."

As soon as he spoke those words, he let go of my hand and stood there with a smile on his face. The boy shouted from the stairs above, "What are you waiting for? Let's go." I ran up the stairs and joined them. We almost exited the place when we heard a loud sound coming from outside the place, like a growl. We froze the instant we heard it. The know-it-all boy seemed to be surprised too. The monk seeing our condition shouted from the bottom, "Don't worry about it. It's just our security system."

We went through the cave back to the doorway which was still completely sealed. Anita brought her hand with the relic towards the door and that seemed to do the trick. The door began to slide open. But that meant going out into the cold again. The boy held both of our hands and guided us back to the spaceship.

We went back to the bridge of the spaceship. "One down, two to go," I said. "Well actually," the boy showed a ring on his finger similar to Anita's and said, "I already kind of have the Relic of Space." I had no idea why I didn't notice it before. "But how did you get it? Don't you have to be chosen as a bearer and all that," enquired Anita. "Yeah," said the boy, "And this Relic chose me somehow." There was a genuine look of surprise on his face when he watched his own ring.

I wanted to ask him about what the monk told me at the end. I said to the boy, "Hey can we talk for a minute?" "Sure," he said. "I mean can we talk alone for a bit," I added. Anita frowned at us as we went to the med bay. I told him, "The monk said something about deceiving the bearer of time, death and torment and something like that." The boy repeated exactly what the monk had said earlier. "Yeah, what is it," I asked. The boy answered, "A curse, associated with the Relic of Time. One of the previous bearers was betrayed by his own friend resulting in his death. The Relic sensed the feeling of betrayal in his dying moments and took a curse upon itself. From the next bearer onwards, the one whom the bearer trusts the most gets this warning." I looked at her, standing at a distance trying to figure out what we were discussing. She looked away and pretended to study the spaceship when she saw me looking at her. "Don't worry, I know you won't betray her, and that's all that matters," he said.

We got back to the bridge when Anita asked me, "What was so important that you had to leave me out of it?" Confused about whether lying to her would count as deception, I decided to tell her everything. When I told her about the 'trusting the most' part, she blushed, so I quickly changed the subject. "Where should we go next," I asked the boy. "Back to your house," he said. Great! I left Kolkata for the first time on a flight and would be returning on a spaceship. Yeah, it was really messed up. "But why," I asked. "Well, because the Relic of Knowledge is in your laptop," he answered. But how could a Relic be in a laptop? I asked him this question. He said, "The Relics can disguise themselves as anything and what's a better place to hide information and be close to the next bearer than hiding it in between more information." "But I have had access to my laptop for so many years. If it had chosen me as its next bearer, why didn't it transform into a ring," I asked. "It wasn't the right time for you. And it's a good thing that it didn't. Otherwise, the whole laptop would have transformed," he said. Anita and I both asked, "So what do we do?" He explained, "The relic will be a simple text file with an unusually large file size in your personal directory. Just copy it into a flash drive and bring it here. And after you copy the file, make sure not to touch the flash drive directly, or it would transform into the ring instantly, and we don't want to attract unwanted attention to ourselves, especially not in your house. Let's go, time's a-wastin'."

I really wanted to fly the spaceship again when we weren't being chased by fighter jets. So I ran towards the front and sat down on the seat which appeared when I wanted it to. The controls appeared in front of me just like it did before. The boy whispered something to Anita to which she laughed and said, "What are you talking about?". She took a seat which appeared beside me after she examined the seat very carefully making sure it was real.

The controls appeared in front of her too and I taught her how to fly the spaceship, which was quite ironic because it was only a few hours back that I had to learn it myself. The boy, looking at the both of us flying his spaceship, took a seat behind us.

CHAPTER EIGHT

Appearances are Deceptive

We flew the spaceship high up and were quite surprised to see some footprints near the place where the ship was on the ground. We were certain they were not human. Perhaps they belonged to the security system the old monk was talking about, we thought.

We decided to leave the thought at that and proceed to the second phase of our plan. It all seemed to be really easy, too easy to be very honest, I thought to myself. Nevertheless, when we were so high up in the atmosphere that we could see the whole of my hometown Kolkata at once, we moved down towards my home. It almost felt like zooming in on an online map save for the fact that it was very real and terrifying, the roads and buildings becoming larger every second, that is until I reduced our velocity and were hovering about a hundred metres above my house.

The boy rushed towards my controls and switched something on saying, "Almost forgot. That's better." The voice in the spaceship announced, "Invisibility Shield now activated." I was quite amazed at the various abilities of the ship but what can you expect from a spaceship from the future?

I got up from my chair and so did Anita. I was going through the plan once more in my mind when it struck me. What should I tell my parents? How could I explain everything to them? They knew that I would be coming back home from the excursion two days later. I told Anita and the boy about this problem. We all thought about it a bit and the best solution that we could come up with was for me to tell them that the excursion had been cancelled. That would at least give me the time to retrieve the Relic and get out. I could tell them that I had left my luggage outside the apartment and by the time they would realise that there was no luggage, I would be out of the house, probably by giving another excuse.

I was really nervous. "You should be fine. Don't worry," said the boy as I was being lowered down from the spaceship while Anita gave me a thumbs up.

As soon as I was outside the spaceship, I couldn't see the ship any longer. It was as if it wasn't there at all. I stepped off the circular platform that was now on the ground and it went back up. After rising up for some time, the platform too seemed to vanish. I walked up to my apartment. I had left my watch back in Bengaluru when the boy came to my hotel room in the morning. But by the position of the Sun, I deduced that it was around 2 p.m. in the afternoon. I went up the stairs to my house and the most unexpected person was waiting in the front room.

Rahul, my former classmate whom I also met on my flight, was sitting in the front room. My mom came out from the kitchen, probably after hearing my footsteps. "Rahul told me you'd be back soon," she said.

What was he doing here? Wasn't he going to attend some wedding in Bengaluru? And how in the world did he know that I was coming back home?

I had so many questions in my mind. But I decided to stick to the plan as far as possible. As far as I was concerned, the part of the excuse was already sorted. But I could sense that something was wrong. Some things didn't quite add up.

I grinned at Rahul, took some packs of chocolate from the refrigerator and started eating one of them as I was starving. I kept the others in my pocket. Then I went directly to my study room where I had kept my laptop, after telling my mom that I had to check the results of a quiz in which I had participated at the ICI. Yeah, that was the best excuse that I could come up with at the moment.

Rahul seemed to follow me there. His face had a look of suspicion on it. I grabbed a spare flash drive I had lying around on my desk, inserted it into the laptop and turned the laptop on.

"Whatcha doing," interrupted Rahul and sat down beside me after bringing his chair from the front room. "Oh, it's nothing serious. Just checking something," I was stalling as I searched for the Relic when he said, "Give me the Relics or they die." I froze. The pack of chocolate that I was eating dropped from my hand. I looked at him. It was a calm, emotionless face which made his words even more threatening.

"What Relics," I said, my voice shaking. He said, "Come on. Two of your friends are already dead. Let's not play games here. Just give me the Relics and we'll leave peacefully. There's no need for any more deaths." He knew about the Relics and that one of the Conquerors had shot Anita. But that meant only one thing. He was a Conqueror. There was no other possibility. I thought if one of them could shoot an unarmed girl just because she was running into an unauthorised space, he could do anything to get the Relics. Although I felt a bit guilty after contemplating whether it was my acquaintance with him that ultimately resulted in the Conquerors finding him and turning him into one of their own, he was no longer the quiet backbencher I knew.

But I couldn't let my parents die, even if it meant giving him the Relic of Knowledge. "Fine! I only have one of the Relics. I will give it to you. Just leave my family alone," I said. He nodded his head.

I found the hefty text file in my personal directory and moved it to the flash drive. I remembered what the boy had said about not touching the drive with my bare hands, so I pulled out a piece of paper from the printer and took out the flash drive.

I presented it to Rahul who shouted, "Do you think this is a joke? Give me the real Relic or your parents die!" My mom came out of the kitchen due to all the shouting. "What happened? Why are you guys fighting," asked my mom. He answered "Oh, it's nothing. Just two friends having a friendly chat. Isn't it?" He looked at me. I nodded just like you do if someone is pointing a gun at you.

My mom went back to the kitchen. "Now, the Relic." I told him the flash drive was the Relic and would transform once it touched its bearer. I didn't reveal that I was the bearer because he didn't seem to know it and I very much wanted to keep that information from their hive mind.

He took the flash drive from my hand. "Oh, I see... Thank you," he said. He got up from his chair. "Now just be calm, and it'll all be fine," he said as he pulled out a gun from his jeans pocket. I recognised the gun instantly. A shiver went down my spine. I stood up. "You can't do this," I said, "Rahul, if you're there, fight it." He answered, "Oh, don't bother. He won't be able to help you much. Any last words?"

I was probably going to say something dumb when Bam! Rahul fell down on the ground. "That's for shooting me," Anita shouted.

"Are you alright," she said, gasping for breath and holding my 11th-grade Biology textbook in her hand. I had never felt such relief after seeing anyone as I did after I saw her at that moment. The weight of the book was enough to incapacitate him. "Yeah," I said, still looking at Rahul, or whatever he was now, "How did you know I was in danger?" Anita said, "The Relic showed me a vision of this exact moment. Now let's go!" I picked up the flash drive which was lying near Rahul's hand with the paper I had previously used and immediately gave it to Anita lest I should trigger its transformation. She tucked it inside her jeans pocket.

I was walking towards the front room when my mom came out of the kitchen. She shouted at Anita, "What have you done?" I said, "I will explain everything later. Just get him out of the house and close the door." She bent down towards Rahul to check on him while Anita and I ran out.

"Not so fast guys," said my mom, pointing Rahul's gun at us. We froze. I felt a burst of pain and defeat in my heart as I realised that she had already been transformed into a Conqueror, and the pain spread to every inch of my body, filling it with a kind of exhaustion. If Anita had not struck the blow to Rahul's head, I would have probably become one of them too. Anita and I were going to make a run for it when I saw my father climbing up the stairs. "The Relics, please," he said, just as calmly as Rahul did before he was going to shoot me.

"I have an idea. But it may not work, and we may fall to our deaths," Anita whispered into my ears. "Any plan is better than no plan," I said. It was impossible for us to get to the ground floor without getting shot, especially when you live on the third floor. So we decided to make a run for the terrace.

We somehow reached the terrace which was just above us by dodging the bullets fired by my parents. Although I was saving myself, a part of my mind was still comprehending the fact that my parents were dead. It was just yesterday when I saw their concerned but proud faces bidding farewell to me at the airport. And now they were no more.

We ran towards the end of the terrace. My parents were still on the stairs. "Can you bring the ship exactly there," she pointed at a particular point in the air just outside the terrace. "How long will it take, I mean down to the seconds," she asked. I deduced that she was communicating with the boy somehow.

"We need to jump," she said to me, as I heard my mom coming out of the entrance to the terrace. "That's your idea," I exclaimed. "Do you trust me," she said to me. To be honest, although I had known her for only one day, I felt she was the only person I could trust with my life, especially after what I had just witnessed. After all, she had just saved me from getting killed by Rahul. I clasped her hand and said, "Yes, I do." She muttered to herself, "Well that makes one of us." We climbed up the terrace wall together. She said, "Just close your eyes immediately after we jump. Ready?" I nodded my head.

I heard a gunshot but it was too late. We had already jumped. I couldn't see anything. I only felt the fast wind blowing past my face and Anita's tight grip on my hand which I thought would leave me with bruises for at least a week. But it was no more than two seconds before I felt that I had hit the ground. I was assured by Anita's extremely loud 'Woo-hoo!' that we were still alive and that it was quite safe to open my eyes.

"Where's the Relic," the boy came running towards me. I realised that I was back on the spaceship. Although I had just arrived there from my actual house, the spaceship seemed more like a home to me, perhaps because the people who made my house my home were now no more.

I felt a pain near the front of my head, which grew intense every second. I heard the boy and Anita shouting but everything appeared to become so dizzy. If only I could take a minute of rest on the ground, I thought to myself.

I woke up and found myself on one of the MedBeds. Anita was there, sitting on a chair beside me. As soon as I woke up, Anita stood up, rubbed her eyes a bit while looking away and said in a shaky voice, "How are you now?" I didn't feel any pain in my head anymore, not even the slightest headache. I said this to her to which she replied, "Good. You should rest for a while." She almost ran out of the med bay. Soon, the boy came in. "You alright," he asked me. I nodded my head. "Was she crying," I asked him. "Yeah," he said, "While appreciating the technology of the MedBed I told her that had it not been for tech from my time, you would have died. And she kind of blames herself for your being like this. So..." I protested, "But she saved us both. How did she do it anyway?" "She's a genius," said the boy, "She made me calculate exactly how much time it would take for me to go to the place she showed me just outside your terrace. After you both reached that exact position, I started moving the ship and she made you travel with her exactly that amount of time into the future using her Relic. As a result, both of you travelled in time so that the ship would then be at that particular place to catch you both. But you fell head first and fractured your skull." I frowned at him. He said, "Don't worry, you're quite fine right now."

I suddenly remembered my parents. He must have understood that as he said, "I'm really sorry about your Mom and Dad. I know what it's like to see your parents turn into them." That made me really angry. He was a robot. He didn't have any parents. How could he understand my pain? It was he who dragged me into all of this mess. I didn't ask to be a part of this fight. I was almost ready to punch him in the face when he looked around and said, "We're here."

CHAPTER NINE

TRUTH AND FAREWELL

He was walking out of the med bay when I called him, "Where is here? And what's our next move?" He smiled a bit, with a sorrowful expression on his face, "First let's take a walk outside, shall we? And bring Anita with you." He went outside the med bay and immediately came back and said, "Oh, I almost forgot. Your jackets should be in the Vaults. Take them with you." He went back out. I got out of the MedBed and stood up. Other than being a bit disoriented, I was quite fine. I went out of the med bay only to find Anita facing a corner in the control room.

"Hey, it wasn't your fault," I said. "Of course it was," protested Anita, still sobbing, "You shouldn't have trusted me." "I'm really fine. See," I said, trying to console her. "You could have died because of me," she shouted. I said, "But I didn't. And you saved me, from..." I remembered the moment in my house when I realised my parents had the Conquerors inside them activated. "I'm sorry," said Anita. I didn't say anything. It was probably me who got them killed in the first place. What I wouldn't give to hear their loving voice once more, to be hugged by those loving arms,

I thought.

I noticed Anita staring at me, who immediately looked away. "You should probably check up on your parents once," I said to her. "Oh," she sighed, "don't worry about them. I'm sure that they are fine." "Still," I said. "My parents," she said, anger written all over her face, "They don't care about me. They just put me in a boarding school when I was five and I only see them once a year. I don't even know where they are right now, let alone the Conquerors." I realised that the emotion visible on her face was more of loneliness and helplessness that she might have felt throughout her life. I gave her one of the two packs of chocolate that I had in my pocket. She took it and smiled, "You know, you two are the first real family that I have had in a very long time," she said.

"By the way, how exactly did you travel in time," I enquired. She said, "I don't really know. I kind of wanted it to happen and it did. It's really quite strange to be honest."

We looked at each other for a moment without speaking when I broke the ice by saying, "We should probably go. He's waiting outside. And he told us to bring some jackets for some reason." Anita frowned a bit and said, "Where will we get jackets here?" I told her about the thing he said about some vault, but I didn't know where it was and neither did she. I had a bizarre idea. I said, "Spaceship, can you please show us the way to the Vault?" "Sure," a voice announced, "Please follow me." The lights of the walls to a particular way turned green. We followed them until we were in a room full of closed lockers.

Two of the vaults were open and parts of jackets were visible. One of them was a blue one and the other yellow. I wore the blue jacket while Anita reached for the other. We travelled back to the bridge and then to the exit platform.

The platform started to descend as soon as both of us stood on it. I was wondering what was so important that the boy put our plan, which was supposedly his entire mission, aside and landed the ship just before its completion.

As we got down to the ground, I understood why the boy had told us to wear the jackets. Even with the jackets on, we could feel the freezing cold wind slowing down our blood. But all this seemed to vanish as soon as I saw the sky. It was a stunning view. I had always wanted to see the Northern Lights. I never told anyone about this desire of mine. And the boy brought me to the one place I had always wanted to be.

I saw the boy standing in the distance. We walked up to him and stood there for a while. I felt something in the pocket of my jacket; it was some kind of piece of paper. I reached inside to bring it out. As soon as I saw what it was, I felt a chill down my spine. It was as if the cold outside intensified a thousand times. I showed it to Anita and her face turned pale.

It was just a picture, but I felt it had just slapped me. The picture was of the boy but with Anita's and my hands over his shoulders. We were much older, perhaps in our late twenties. We all were smiling. We looked really happy. There were other guys too just behind us, all happy faces. The words 'My Family' were written on the back of the picture. It was my handwriting.

I kept on staring at the picture for a full minute when the boy said, looking at the sky, "This was your dying wish, your greatest regret. Despite all your journeys, you always wanted to see the Northern Lights with her. But it never really happened." He looked at Anita. He went on, "I said I knew what it was like to lose your parents to the Conquerors. It's because I lost my own. I saw them chasing me and trying to kill me, just like you. So, before I complete my final mission, I decided to complete a more personal one. Hello Dad, Mom." Tears rolled down his face as he spoke. "But you said the greatest minds of the Earth created you," I said. "Yeah," he said, "I did. That was the truth. You found the picture I see." Taking the picture from my hand he said, "This was our crew. You personally selected them for the Resistance's best ship, Eternity. You were our captain, our inspiration and Anita was your first officer. But above all, you both had brilliant minds. You created me with the help of the Designers. You kept on fighting, until she died." He looked at Anita and then me, "After she had become a Conqueror, you were shot with the activator. At the same time, we came to know of the fourth Relic which was in the possession of the Conquerors and had turned an entire platoon into Conquerors at once. You knew you didn't have much time. So just before you became one of them, you gave me this mission and this ship."

He paused for a second and then said, "My journey with you has almost come to an end. This is the last time I will be seeing you." He was trying to hold back his tears and to be honest, so was I. He came towards us and hugged us both. "Thank you, for everything."

After a minute, he pulled away, wiped his face with his hands, took a deep breath and said to Anita, "You still have his Relic?" She pulled out the flash drive from her pocket and held it in her hand. I picked it up when it started to glow. The intensity started increasing, just like it did with Anita's Relic, but this time, the light was blue in colour. I could see the brightness increasing so much that I could hardly see anything except the Relic, but the brightness didn't seem to hurt my eyes. I saw the flash drive turning into a ball of pure blue light and then it changed into a ring, still just as bright. The brightness then started to decrease gradually until a ring was left behind in my hands. It was similar to Anita's but instead of the straight groove, this one had an engraving of two lines wound around each other. I wore it on my finger and looked at the boy. He was smiling proudly.

"We should go back; complete the mission," said the boy. Anita and I were walking back towards our ship when the boy called from behind, "Anita, can I talk to you for a minute?" She went back to the boy. I stood there looking at them. He explained something to her which made her look at me. But she was staring at me with a face that expressed tremendous sadness and despair. She said something back to him, nodding her head in disagreement. The boy placed his hand over her shoulder and told her something again. He explained something to her for a full minute after which Anita looked down.

They started walking towards me when I started heading back to the ship. Once we were all back on the bridge, Anita and I took off our jackets and went towards the controls at the front. The boy said to me, "Permission to fly the ship for one last time, Captain?" "Of course," I said, though not fully understanding why it would be his last time flying the ship. But I didn't ask him that. He took a seat and the control panel appeared right in front of him. We sat down trusting the ship; that a chair would appear where we were. Thankfully, it did.

We went up high into the atmosphere and then we were heading back towards India, to Bengaluru, to the ICI. We landed near the ICI buildings. I didn't know what we were supposed to do next, so I followed him out of the ship. He stopped after walking some steps towards the main entrance of the ICI and faced us and said, "The fourth Relic is in there."

I asked him, "What's our next move?" He replied, "The only way to destroy the fourth Relic is for me to take the permission of the other two Relic bearers and draw power from their Relics to overload my internal nuclear reactor and then use that to destabilise the fourth Relic so much that it explodes, taking down at least the Conqueror Queen. Both the active and the dormant Conquerors would naturally die off within a few years." But that meant he was going to commit a suicide bombing. But at that time, with my parents dead and after knowing his real identity, I felt that he was the only family that I had left, albeit from the future. I protested, "No, there has to be another way. I can't lose you too. Not after everything you have told me about our future. And won't it kill everyone in this city?" "The Relic will explode, not my reactor. The radius of the blast will not be more than this building - enough to kill all the active Conquerors inside. Look, I was made for this. Don't worry everything will be okay in the end. And don't worry about the ship. I have already programmed it. It will stay hidden till the time is right."

Saying this, he held both of our hands and asked us, "Do I have your permission to use the power of your relics to prevent the extinction of the humans?" Anita and I paused for a second, looking at his face, full of optimism and said, "Yes." As soon as we did, we started to lift up off the ground. The boy started to take long and deep breaths. Some armed guards came out. They started mindlessly shooting at us just like before, but this time the bullets just bounced off some kind of energy shield around the three of us.

After two minutes, the boy opened his eyes and we descended onto the ground. It almost felt like he was glowing. All the guards concentrated their fire on him as if they couldn't see us at all. But I didn't complain as the bullets didn't seem to affect him at all. He entered the building quite easily after hitting all of the guards at once with a bolt of electricity. I suddenly realised I had forgotten to ask him the most obvious question you ask a person after you meet them. "Hey," I called out to him, "We didn't get to know your name by the way." He looked back at us, smiled cryptically and then kept on walking.

Soon, we heard the fire alarm ringing and numerous people started coming out. Almost all the people had come out but none of the guards were to be seen. We stood there for half a minute more when Anita suddenly said to me, with the same sense of urgency you feel when you have too much to say in a very little amount of time, "Whatever happens after this, just don't worry. Everything will be alright. Okay?" She held my hand tightly.

I couldn't understand what she was talking about and why on earth was everybody telling me not to worry? Suddenly the whole ICI building exploded. Anita let go of my hands and held hers together. I could feel the heat of the explosion in my hands and face when suddenly, everything became bright white. I closed my eyes due to the dazzling light everywhere.

When I opened my eyes, I was back in my house, in my bed, my parents sitting beside me. I thought that I was dead, or was I dreaming? No, I didn't have the imagination to dream up such an insane story, I must have died, I thought. "Just tell me the truth," I said to my Mom, "Am I dead?" "No! You just had a bad dream, sweetheart," she said, "But you should watch the news. I don't think you will be having that ICI excursion anytime soon." I didn't care at first. It felt so good to hug my parents once more. I almost cried in their arms. I got out of bed and went to the TV. In addition to the fact that I was still wearing the shiny black ring with wavy lines encircling it, the headline in big bold letters made me certain that I didn't dream up the entire story. "Indian Cosmological Institute Destroyed Completely; Terrorist Attack suspected, 49 Dead," read the news. Then all of a sudden, it struck me, that although our mission had been a success and I remembered everything, I wouldn't have met Anita had it not been for the excursion. And now that the excursion was cancelled, I had a thousand questions in my mind. Did she even remember the incidents and all the things the three of us went through together? Would I ever get to meet her again?

9 798888 497692

Printed by Libri Plureos GmbH in Hamburg, Germany